Fertile Heart:

The Magical Story of How YOU Were Made

By Debra Doubrava, PhD

Illustrated by Nicole Smith-Merry, MS & Julia Parker

Balboa Press books may be ordered through booksellers or by contacting:

Balboa Press
A Division of Hay House
1663 Liberty Drive
Bloomington, IN 47403
www.balboapress.com
844-682-1282

asifbook.com

Illustrated by Nicole Smith-Merry, MS & Julia Parker

ISBN: 979-8-7652-4148-6 (sc)
ISBN: 979-8-7652-4149-3 (e)

Library of Congress Control Number: 2023908087

Print information available on the last page.

Balboa Press rev. date: 07/10/2023

BALBOA.PRESS
A DIVISION OF HAY HOUSE

Foreword

As a psychologist with over 20 years of experience helping prospective parents prepare to use fertility assistance in their quest to have children, I was thrilled to see *Fertile Love: The Magical Story of How YOU Were Made* (2022) and now *Fertile Heart: The Magical Story of How YOU Were Made* (2023) by Debra Doubrava, PhD. I recommend the reading of books as a helpful way to introduce children to their own story. These books, with their simple narratives and whimsical, brightly colored illustrations, offer an opportunity for parents and children to have a gradually more detailed discussion of the fertility journey and the magic and love that helped bring a very special being into the world.

— Joan L. Bitzer, Psychologist

Fertile (adj.) bearing in abundance.

*"Making the decision to have a child is momentous.
It is to decide forever to have your heart
go walking around outside your body."*

-Elizabeth Stone

Dedicated to our loved ones and
to families everywhere
who are made by magical decisions
and fertile hearts.
May YOU all live abundantly ever after!!!

Once upon a time (by the way
many truly magical stories begin this way
and this truly IS a magical story)...
there was a person who had a full
life and a fertile heart.

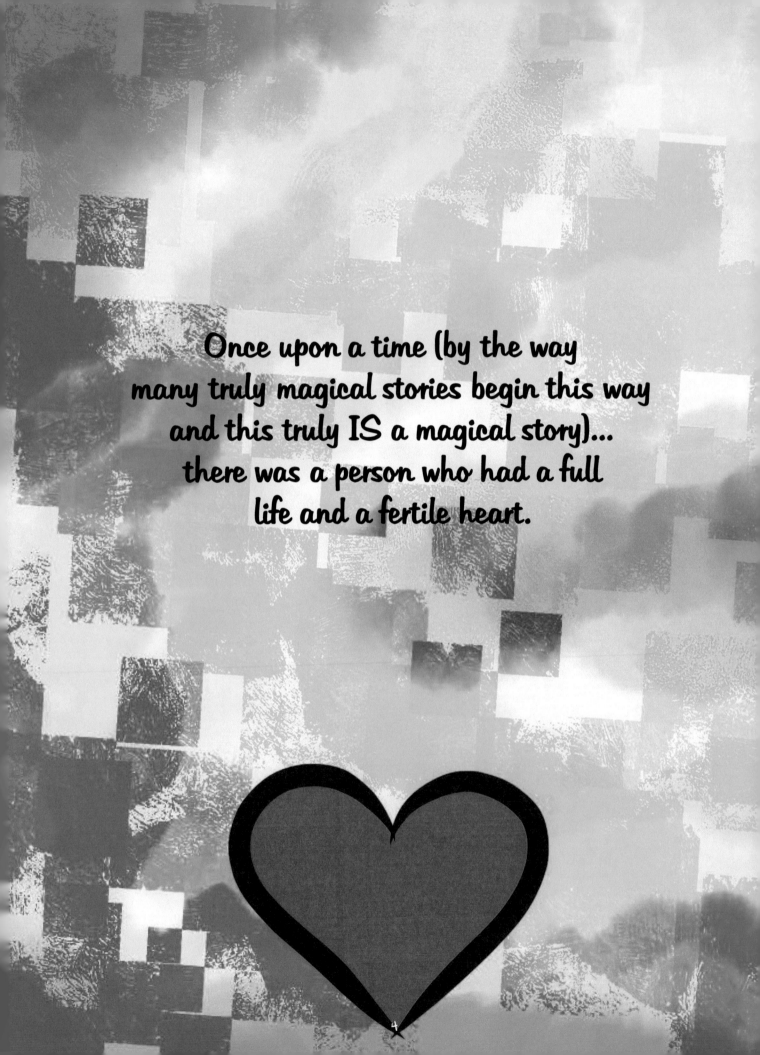

The person spent their days
doing meaningful heart work & play,
but their life journey felt empty
in one truly big way...

They knew they wanted a baby
to share their fertile heart with.

But though their life was full of love and light,
the person did not have the key ingredients
all on their own to get the baby recipe right.

The person felt sad and frustrated
wondering if they should let go
of their fertile dream.

Until one day, they had a magical
knowing that they needed help
AND could *borrow* ingredients to make the baby
who was knocking on the door
to their fertile heart.

And so, with courage and fertile hope,
the person asked for help from angels
who were always destined to be
part of this magical story.

And YOU were made!!!

And the person felt blessed and grateful
to be your parent and like
all was right with the world.

And your life will be full.
And your heart will be fertile.

And you will live

abundantly ever after knowing...

You are MAGICAL.

You are wanted.

You are loved.

THE END

(Many magical stories end this way,
but this is not THE END...
it's YOUR beginning.)

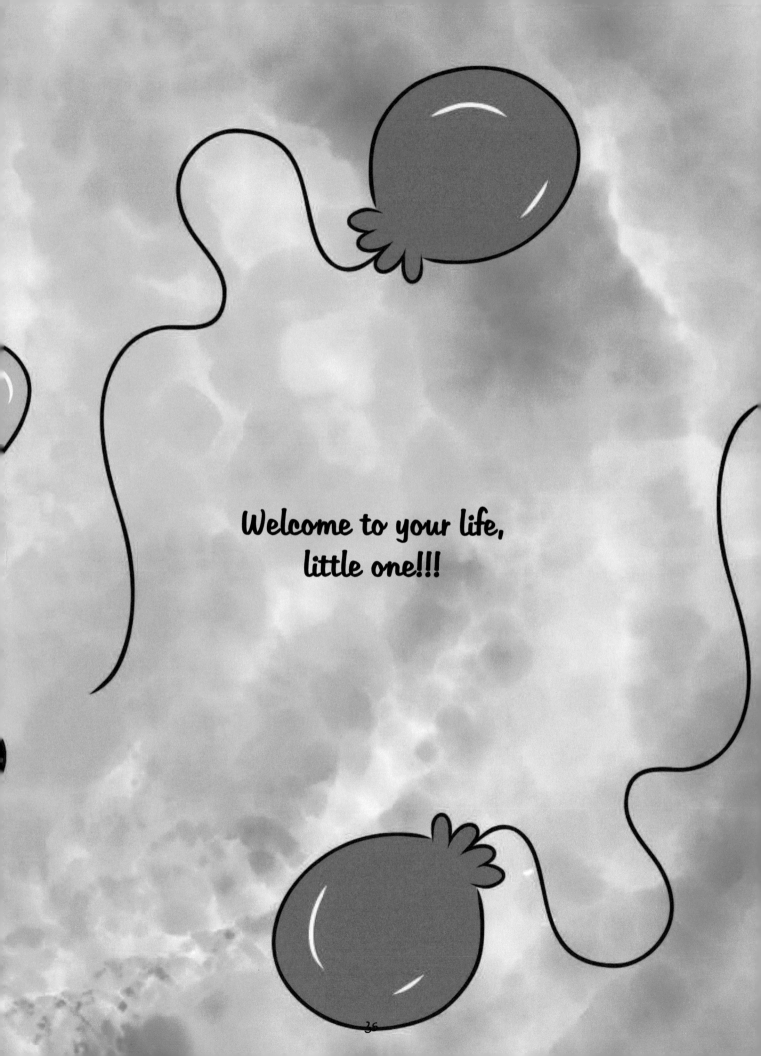

Welcome to your life,
little one!!!

Dear Parents:

You did it!!! Your dream came true to make the baby who was knocking on the door to your fertile heart.

Everyone wants to know where they came from ...And what a truly magical story you have to share with your little one!!!

The abbreviated edition that follows is an opportunity for you to creatively personalize this book for your child's delight and information.

Enjoy!

Peace and love,

Dr. Debbie

Fertile Heart: The Magical Story of How YOU Were Made in 3 Creative Chapters

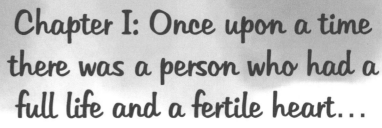

Chapter I: Once upon a time there was a person who had a full life and a fertile heart...
And they knew they wanted a baby to share their fertile heart with.

Your parent:

Three cool things about your parent and their life journey:

1.

2.

3.

Thank you, Angel Helpers, for your help in this magical story:

Chapter II:
And YOU were made!!!

Date and Place of Birth:

YOU were named:

Because:

Three fun facts about your birth story and the making of YOU:

1.

2.

3.

Chapter III: And YOU will live abundantly ever after knowing...
You are magical. You are wanted. You are loved.

Celebrations of YOU:

Your circle of love includes:

Three magical phrases to describe your spirit:

1.

2.

3.

This is not THE END...it's YOUR beginning.

Your parent truly loves this photo of YOU!!!

Epilogue: Words of fertile love
and abundant wisdom
from your blessed and grateful parent
to YOU on your life journey.

Dear

Printed in the United States
by Baker & Taylor Publisher Services